Robert L. C. White, Knights of Pythias, Tennessee Grand
Lodge

Offical Digest of the Grand Lodge Knights of Pythias

of the state of Tennessee

Robert L. C. White, Knights of Pythias, Tennessee Grand Lodge

Offical Digest of the Grand Lodge Knights of Pythias
of the state of Tennessee

ISBN/EAN: 9783337223298

Printed in Europe, USA, Canada, Australia, Japan

Cover: Foto ©Andreas Hilbeck / pixelio.de

More available books at **www.hansebooks.com**

OFFICIAL DIGEST

OF THE

Grand Lodge Knights of Pythias

OF THE

STATE OF TENNESSEE,

————

By R. L. C. WHITE, P. G. C., S. R.

————

PRINTED BY ORDER OF THE GRAND LODGE.
1885.

Official Announcement.

OFFICE OF THE GRAND CHANCELLOR,
PULASKI, TENN., Sept. 1, 1885,

P. P. XXII.

The grand lodge, at its 1885 session, having instructed the grand chancellor to prepare or have prepared a revised edition of our grand lodge digest, I immediately requested Past Grand Chancellor R. L. C. White to undertake the revision. By great labor, he presents thus early what appears, from limited examination, to be a complete work of its kind. From my knowledge of his ability to do the work exactly correct, and trusting confidently in his fidelity to do it justly, I have no hesitation in committing it to the Knights of Pythias of Tennessee as a trustworthy guide to the law; and it is hereby promulgated as the only authorized and official digest for this grand jurisdiction. I recommend a careful study of its contents, and urge that every member of the order in Tennessee provide himself with a copy.

LAPS. D. McCORD,
Grand Chancellor.

To the Memory
of
William Bryce Thompson,
Author of the First Digest,
This Work Is Dedicated
by One
Who Loved Him Well.

At the Outer Door.

Page

THE GRAND LODGE:

Composition and powers 15
Meetings 17
Quorum and voting 17
Officers 18
Representatives and alternates 23
Committees 24
Mileage and per diem 24
Absentees 24
Regalia 25
Conduct of business 25
Grand lodge dues 27
Amendments 28
Miscellaneous 29

THE SUBORDINATE LODGE:

Meetings and quorum 31
Deputy grand chancellor 32
Past chancellors 35
Officers in general 37
Installation 39
Honors 42
Sitting past chancellor 42
Chancellor commander 44
Committees 44
Conduct of business 45
Lodge finances 46

THE SUBORDINATE LODGE (Continued): Page

Benefits 47
Dispensations 48
Secret work 49
Petitions 50
Rank fees 50
Ballot on petitions 51
By-laws 52
Miscellaneous 53
New lodges 53
Defunct lodges 55

THE INDIVIDUAL MEMBER:

Admission 57
Pages and esquires 59
S. A. P. W. 60
Benefits 60
Relief 61
Assessments 62
Fines 62
Absentees 63
Uniform 63
Offences, trials and punishments 64
Appeals 64
Cards and shields 65
Suspension 69
Reinstatement 70

ALPHABETICAL INDEX 73

In the Ante-Room.

At the recent session of the grand lodge, the appended resolution was adopted:

Resolved, that the grand chancellor be and he is hereby instructed to prepare, or have prepared under his direction, a revised edition of our grand lodge digest, embracing all enactments and decisions of this body to the present session; and, when prepared, it shall be printed and bound, and disposed of by the grand keeper of records and seal at such price as will be sufficient to reimburse the grand lodge for the expense incurred. (Jour. 1885, 305-6.)

Immediately after the close of the session, the writer was requested by the grand chancellor to undertake the work of revision. With considerable reluctance, he consented to do so. This reluctance was not occasioned by unwillingness to perform, for the " good of the order," any labor of which he was considered capable: it arose from the fact that, while the matter of the digest which he was asked to revise was admirably prepared, the method of its arrangement did not meet his approbation; and he was of

2

course aware that, if his work was to be
merely a revision, the plan of the existing
digest must necessarily be followed. The
method alluded to—that of arbitrary alphabetical arrangement of topics—has been em-
ployed by the authors of all digests that the
writer has seen; but it seems to him that
this plan has absolutely nothing to recommend it except "the poor excuse of custom,"
while its disadvantages are many and patent.

Recognizing the fact that the end which
the grand lodge desired to attain was simply
the production of a digest which should em-
brace its legislation to date, and that either
a revision of the old digest or an entirely
new work would be satisfactory if this result were achieved, it was finally determined,
after mature deliberation, to undertake the
latter.

This decision has rendered practicable an
enlargement of the scope of the work, by the
addition of a new feature, the value of which,
it is believed, will be readily recognized by
those who have occasion to consult our printed codes.   Our constitution and general
laws are the result of the legislative accre-
tions of many years, each successive grand

lodge having made such additions as seemed proper. Unfortunately, many of these additions, having been made without due consideration, did not always find the most appropriate places in the instruments into which they were injected—some of them gaining lodgment in positions in which no one would ever think of seeking for them— and the consequence is that it is frequently a matter of considerable difficulty to exhume the constitutional provision on a given subject. An attempt has been made, in this digest, to obviate this difficulty by the inclusion of a summary of the principal provisions of the constitution and the general laws. This summary has been embraced in the body of the work, so that all the laws, whether constitutional or statutory, on any point will be found grouped together.

The plan of this digest, which has been adopted in preference to the forced A. B. C. arrangement of similar works, is believed to be unique. The matter has been divided, as seemed natural and logical, into three principal parts, relating respectively to the grand lodge, to the subordinate lodge and to the individual member. Each of these divisions has been subdivided under appropriate heads, the topic treated being placed under what seem to the author its proper title. Repetition of sections under different heads has been avoided by copious cross references in the alphabetical index at the end of the book, consultation of which will enable the enquirer to find what the law of the grand lodge of Tennessee is on any subject concerning which it has legislated.

Many of the "decisions" of our grand chancellors have consisted merely of repetitions of, or references to, the provisions of the supreme law. Except in a few instances in which their insertion seemed necessary to a clear comprehension of the subject, these decisions have been omitted, as having no place in a grand lodge digest. Otherwise, this work is believed to be thorough and complete; and the enquirer who fails to find in the index some reference to a subject may be sure that it is one which the supreme lodge has treated explicitly or the grand lodge of Tennessee has not treated at all.

Those who have occasion to consult this book should bear in mind the fact that a digest is not THE LAW, but merely AN INDEX TO THE LAW. The quotations here given are believed to be as full as will be needed for the great majority of cases; but, whenever any doubt remains, it will always be best to refer to the original authorities cited.

The enlarged scope of this digest has of course involved much more labor than would have been necessary had only a revision of the first digest been undertaken. The work has been done in such intervals of leisure as the author has been able to purloin from engrossing engagements—but it has been "a labor of love," and its result is here presented, as a "free will offering," to the Knights of Pythias of Tennessee.

The seeker for Pythian knowledge, being now "fully equipped" with the necessary preliminary information, is cordially invited to "work his way" within.

R. L. C. W.

Lebanon, Tenn., August, 1885.

OFFICIAL DIGEST.

I.--THE GRAND LODGE.

Composition and Powers.

1. The grand lodge is composed of all past grand chancellors and past chancellors in good standing in their respective lodges.

Con., ii, 1.

2. The rank of past chancellor shall never be conferred on anyone except—

(*a*) A knight who has served as chancellor commander to the close of a term;

(*b*) A knight who has been selected by vote of his lodge to receive the rank, on account of the retiring chancellor commander being already a past chancellor;

(*c*) The first sitting past chancellor of a new lodge;

(*d*) A knight designated, at the institution of a new lodge, to receive the rank.

Con., ii, 2.

3. A past chancellor, before admission to the grand lodge, must present a certificate of the prescribed form from his lodge.

Con., ii, 3.

4. The grand lodge has the sole power to grant charters to subordinate lodges in the state of Tennessee, and to suspend or revoke them.

Con., iii.

5. The grand lodge has the right and power of hearing all appeals.

Con., iii.

6. An appeal from the action of a subordinate lodge should be taken directly to the grand lodge, and not to the grand chancellor.

Jour. 1883, pp. 68, 92.

7. Such appeal, however, if received by the grand chancellor, may be treated as a request for an official decision, and his opinion expressed accordingly.

Jour. 1883, pp. 68, 92.

8. The grand lodge invests the grand

chancellor with full power during its recess.

Con., iii.

Meetings.

9. The sessions of the grand lodge are held annually, on the third Tuesday in May, at 10 o'clock A. M., at a place selected at the previous session. If no place be chosen, it shall meet at Nashville.

Con., v.

10. All invitations for the session of the grand lodge must be presented on the first day of the session, and referred to the committee on mileage and per diem, which shall report the comparative expense of holding the session at the various places.

Jour. 1882, p. 37.

11. It is recommended that subordinate lodges, situated at places where sessions of the grand lodge are held, do not provide any extraordinary entertainment for the grand lodge.

Jour. 1884, p. 205.

Quorum and Voting.

12. Representatives of a majority of the active lodges constitute a quorum in the grand lodge.   Con., xi, 1.

3

13. Each past grand chancellor, who is in good standing in his subordinate lodge, is entitled to one vote in the grand lodge.

Con., ii, 1.

14. Except in the election of grand officers, only representatives, grand officers and past grand chancellors can vote.

Con., xi, 2.

15. It requires a two-thirds vote to appropriate money, amend the constitution or remove a grand officer. All other questions in the grand lodge are decided by a majority.

Con., xi, 3.

16. Five representatives may demand the yeas and nays.

Con., xi, 4.

17. Grand lodge officers can not vote on amendments of the general laws.

Jour. 1879, p. 365.

This ruling was reversed by the supreme lodge, on appeal. (See supreme lodge journal 1880, p. 2035.)

Officers.

18. The officers of the grand lodge are:

(*a*) The sitting past grand chancellor (who is the retiring grand chancellor);

(*b*) The grand chancellor;

(*c*) The grand vice chancellor;

(*d*) The grand prelate;

(*e*) The grand keeper of records and seal;

(*f*) The grand master of exchequer;

(*g*) The grand master at arms;

(*h*) The grand inner guard; and

(*i*) The grand outer guard—

who are elected at each annual session; and

(*j*) Two supreme representatives, who are elected for four years. A majority vote is required to elect.

Con., vi, 1; vii, 1.

19. The election of grand officers shall take place on the last day of the session.

Jour. 1873, p. 45.

This rule was afterwards rescinded, and the election now occurs at the pleasure of the grand lodge, the time being usually fixed in advance by resolution.

Jour. 1880, p. 415.

20. Each past chancellor, who is in good standing in his subordinate lodge, is entitled

to one vote in the election of grand officers.
Con., ii, 1.

21. In the election of grand officers, each lodge is entitled to a number of votes equal to the number of its past chancellors and representatives.
Con., vii, 2.

22. In the election of grand officers, each representative is entitled to cast one vote for each past grand chancellor, as well as one for every past chancellor, in good standing in his lodge, who is is not present.
Jour. 1882, p. 32.

23. In the election of grand officers, each lodge is entitled to one vote for each past grand chancellor and past chancellor who is actually a member of the lodge when the vote is cast, as shown by the official roster.
Jour. 1884, p. 197.

24. The last business before closing shall be the installation of officers.
Con., xvi, 9.

25. No one is eligible to office in the grand lodge who can not be present at the installation.
Jour. 1875, p. 179.

26. The place of any grand officer elect who is absent at the time of installation must immediately be filled by election.

Con:, vii, 4.

27. Any member of the order who solicits votes for himself or for any other nominee for a grand lodge office shall be suspended for not less than six nor more than twelve months.

Con., vii, 5.

28. Duties of officers prescribed.

Con., vi, 2-11.

29. All vacancies in grand lodge offices (except that of grand chancellor) shall be filled by election by a majority of the representatives, the grand chancellor nominating.

Con., vi, 13.

30. A grand officer is not deprived of his rights as such by the surrender of the charter of the subordinate lodge of which he was a member.

Jour. 1877, p. 275.

31. A grand officer may be removed for improper conduct or neglect of duty, by a two-thirds vote of the grand lodge, after trial. A grand officer or member of a committee so offending may be suspended by the grand chancellor until a trial can be had.

Con., ix, 1.

32. No grand officer shall officiate while on trial.

Con., ix, 1.

33. The grand chancellor, the grand keeper of records and seal and the grand master of exchequer constitute a general relief board for the grand jurisdiction.

Jour. 1880, p. 429.

34. The salary and bond of the grand keeper of records and seal shall be determined by the grand lodge from time to time.

Con., vi, 5.

35. The amount of the bond of the grand master of exchequer shall be fixed by the grand lodge from time to time.

Con., vi, 6.

36. The bonds of the retiring grand keeper of records and seal and grand master of exchequer must be filed in the office of the grand keeper of records and seal.

Jour. 1884, p. 202.

37. The report of the supreme represent-atives must be printed and distributed to the lodges as soon after the adjournment of the supreme lodge as practicable.

Jour. 1882, pp. 28-9.

38. The annual reports of the grand chan-cellor and of the grand keeper of records and seal shall be presented in printed form at each session of the grand lodge.

Jour. 1880, p. 428.

Representatives and Alternates.

39. Each subordinate lodge is entitled to one representative to the grand lodge, and to one alternate representative (who repre-sents his lodge in the absence of the repre-sentative). They are elected at ˙ the first stated meeting in December, and must re-ceive a majority of the votes cast   They must present certificates of the prescribed form.

Con. ii, 4.

40. Representatives and alternates must be past chancellors.

G. L., ii, 1.

41. A retiring chancellor commander, who

is not already a past chancellor, is not eligible to election as representative.

Jour. 1883, pp. 69, 96-7.

Committees.

42. List of grand lodge commttees.

Con., vi, 3.

43. All grand lodge committees are appointed at the beginning of each annual session, to serve during the session.

Con., vi, 3.

44. The grand chancellor and the grand keeper of records and seal constitute, ex officio, a committee on subordinate lodge by-laws during the recess of the grand lodge.

Con., xix.

Mileage and Per Diem.

45. The mileage and necessary expenses of grand officers and representatives shall be paid. The mileage shall be three cents, if this will cover actual travelling expenses.

Con., vii, 1.

Absentees.

46. Officers and representatives who fail to answer roll-call at each daily session of the grand lodge, or to report to the grand keeper of records and seal within thirty minutes thereafter, shall not be entitled to per diem for that day's session, unless excused by a unanimous vote of the grand lodge.

Jour. 1873, p. 45.

Regalia.

47. During the sessions of the grand lodge, each representative must wear a collar, with the number of his lodge in metal figures attached thereto.

Jour. 1883, pp. 106-7-8.

Conduct of Business.

48. "Robert's Rules of Order" is the parliamentary guide of the grand lodge.

Con., xv.

49. Order of business prescribed.

Con., xvi.

50. The grand chancellor shall decide without debate all questions of order arising in the grand lodge, from which decision any two members may jointly appeal to the grand lodge.

Con., vi, 3.

51. All documents offered in the grand

4

lôdge, which require to be referred to a committee or to be entered in full on the journal, must be presented in duplicate and on not less than a page of commercial note paper.

Jour. 1884, p. 206.

52. The indefinite postponement of a motion to reconsider action by which a proposed amendment was rejected does not preclude the offering of an identical amendment at the same session, to lie over until the next session.

Jour. 1884, pp. 203-4.

This ruling was sustained by the supreme lodge, on appeal. (See supreme lodge journal 1884, pp. 3038-9.)

53. The fact that no objection is made to the reference to a committee of a resolution or amendment requiring unanimous consent for its consideration at that session, does not impair the right to object to its consideration when the report of the committee is presented.

Jour. 1884, p. 183.

54. The grand lodge will not consider hypothetical questions, unless they come

from a subordinate lodge, under its seal.
Jour. 1879, p. 371.

Grand Lodge Dues.

55. The semi-annual per capita tax shall be fixed at each session of the grand lodge, by a two thirds vote.

Con., viii, 1.

56. Lodges instituted within less than one month of the close of a term are not liable for per capita tax for that term.

Jour. 1874, p. 106.

57. Such lodges must, however, pay per capita tax on those of their members who where admitted by card from lodges in this jurisdiction, and who would have been subject to the tax in the lodges from which they withdrew.

Jour. 1874, pp. 76, 92.

58. Subordinate lodges shall pay such tax on each rank conferred as may be fixed from time to time by the grand lodge.

Jour. 1876, pp. 220, 229-30.

59. The tax on ranks levied by the grand lodge takes effect in each lodge from and after the meeting at which the representative makes his report to the lodge—provided that he makes his report at the first regular meeting after the adjournment of the grand lodge.

Jour. 1877, pp. 245, 272, 275.

60. New lodges are exempt from the payment of rank tax on the first fifteen members initiated.

Jour. 1880, pp. 426-7.

61. A lodge failing to pay its grand lodge dues within thirty days after the end of a term may forfeit its representation in the next session of the grand lodge.

Con., viii, 1.

62. The S. A. P. W. shall not be communicated to a lodge which has not paid its grand lodge dues; and a lodge thus delinquent shall not be allowed a vote in the grand lodge. A lodge six months in arrears shall forfeit its charter.

G. L., x, 3.

Amendments.

63. The constitution of the grand lodge may be amended by a two-thirds vote; but amendments proposed must lie over from one annual session until the next, unless

unanimous consent be given for their consideration at the session at which they are
offered.

Con., xx.

64. The general laws for the government
of subordinate lodges may be amended by
a two-thirds vote; but amendments proposed must lie over from one annual session
until the next, unless the consent of four-
fifths of the representatives present be given
for a suspension of the rules.

G. L., xiii, 2.

For the construction of the word "representatives," as here used, see sec. 17.

Miscellaneous.

65. The frequency with which the secret
work should be exemplified in the grand
lodge is a matter for the decision of each
session of that body.

Jour. 1885, pp. 305-6.

66. The grand keeper of records and seal
must notify each lodge of all suspensions,
other than for non-payment of dues.

Con., vi, 5.

67. The seal of the grand lodge must not

be affixed to any document not emanating from the grand lodge.

Jour. 1880, pp. 391, 425.

68. After the adjournment of the grand lodge, officers shall not be allowed to retain their jewels, except that the grand chancellor may retain his and that of the grand master at arms, giving a receipt to the grand keeper of records and seal; and, in case of loss, he shall be required to replace the same.

Jour. 1883, pp. 100-101.

69. The grand keeper of records and seal must send one copy of the grand lodge journal to each representative, and five to each lodge.

Con., vi, 5.

70. Various blanks are to be furnished to subordinate lodges by the grand keeper of records and seal.

Con., xvii.

71. Prices of supplies.

Con., xii.

II.--THE SUBORDINATE LODGE.

Meetings and Quorum.

72. A subordinate lodge shall never consist of less than seven knights.

G. L., i, 1.

73. Subordinate lodges must meet weekly, unless the grand chancellor grant a dispensation for less frequent meetings.

G. L., i, 1.

74. Special meetings may be called by the chancellor commander at his discretion, or by request of five members. Such meetings must be confined to the business for which they were called.

G. L. i, 3.

75. A lodge failing to hold six consecutive meeting shall forfeit its charter, except in case of epidemic or war.

G. L., i, 2.

76. It is detrimental to the interests of the order for subordinate lodges not to hold regular weekly meetings.

Jour. 1879, p. 372.

77. Seven members constitute a quorum.

G. L., i, 1.

78. If only seven members are present, unanimous consent is required to appropriate money.

G. L., i, 2.

79. When more than seven members of a subordinate lodge are present, a majority vote is sufficient to appropriate money.

Jour. 1876, p. 226.

Deputy Grand Chancellor.

80. A deputy grand chancellor shall be appointed by the grand chancellor for each lodge, to serve for one year. He may be removed by the grand chancellor.

Con., vi, 3.

81. Each lodge shall recommend to the grand chancellor a past chancellor for the position of deputy grand chancellor.

Con., vi, 12.

82. A past chancellor who has not taken the grand lodge rank is eligible to the office of deputy grand chancellor.

Jour. 1883, pp. 68, 96-8.

83. The appointment of the deputy grand chancellor recommended by a subordinate lodge is entirely optional with the grand chancellor. The recommendation is merely advisory.

Jour. 1883, pp. 68, 96-7.

84. The deputy grand chancellor is authority on questions of law referred to him by vote of his lodge, his decision being subject to appeal to the grand chancellor.

G. L., xiii, 1.

85. A deputy grand chancellor must not give official decisions unless requested by vote of the lodge.

Con., vi, 12.

86. All decisions of the deputy grand chancellor must be entered on the records of the lodge.

Con., vi, 12. '

87. The judicial power of a deputy grand chancellor is confined to the uniformity of the work of the order, and he has no power to construe laws, unless specially referred to him by resolution of the lodge, and even then only in strict conformity to the law itself. If a lodge proposes an act which the

5

deputy grand chancellor considers illegal, and the matter is not referred to him officially, he has no more control over it than any other individual member.

Jour. 1881, pp. 448, 483-4.

88. Questions of the construction of law should not be submitted to the grand chancellor until they have been referred to the deputy grand chancellor.

Jour. 1881, pp. 447, 483-4.

89. A deputy grand chancellor may hold a subordinate lodge office.

Jour. 1883, pp. 68, 96-7.
Jour. 1884, pp. 145, 185-6.

90. A deputy grand chancellor must file with the grand chancellor a certificate of good standing, before he can receive the S. A. P. W. for promulgation to his lodge.

Jour. 1881, pp. 454, 503.

91. A deputy grand chancellor must make at least two official visits to his lodge during the year.

Con., vi, 12.

92. Deputy grand chancellors must forward the semi-annual returns to the grand keeper of records and seal within thirty days after the expiration of each term.

Jour. 1883, pp. 100-101.

93. Deputy grand chancellors must report to the grand chancellor, on blanks prepared by the grand keeper of records and seal, the condition of their respective lodges.

Jour. 1881, pp. 481, 489.

94. It is the positive duty of deputy grand chancellors to make report to the grand chancellor of all their official acts, at least one month before the session of the grand lodge.

Jour. 1885, pp. 245, 295.

Past Chancellors.

95. A lodge is entitled to a past chancellor for each official term.

Jour. 1876, p. 227.
Jour. 1883, pp. 69, 96-7.

96. A lodge can not elect a past chancellor to fill a vacancy occasioned by the death, suspension or withdrawal of a past chancellor.

Jour. 1876, pp. 203, 226.

97. At the institution of a new lodge,

three members may be designated for the rank of past chancellor, in addition to the sitting past chancellor.

G. L., ii, 7.

98. A new lodge has the right, under the provisions of art. ii, sec. 7, general laws, to select three knights for the rank of past chancellor, although some of its charter members are already past chancellors.

Jour. 1880, p. 426.

99. A retiring chancellor commander becomes a past chancellor when his successor is installed.

Jour. 1876, pp. 202, 226-7.

100. A chancellor commander who is re-elected becomes a past chancellor when he is installed for his second term.

Jour. 1876, pp. 202, 226-7.

101. The name of the retiring chancellor commander should not be included in the list of past chancellors in the semi-annual returns for the term at the end of which he retired.

Jour. 1882, p. 37.

102. When the retiring chancellor commander is already a past chancellor, the lodge may select a knight to receive the rank of past chancellor.

G. L., ii, 1.

103. Emeritus past chancellors are entiled to all the rights and privileges of past chancellors by service.

Jour. 1879, pp. 328, 362.
Jour. 1882, pp. 8, 30.

104. A resolution which required certain knights, whom the grand lodge had created past chancellors emeritus, to actually receive the rank before they should be considered entitled to the rights and privileges thereof, was declared " illegal and inoperative," as " making undue distinction between past chancellors."

Jour. 1882, pp. 8, 30.

Officers in General.

105. The officers of a subordinate lodge must be elected by ballot at the first stated meetings in June and December respectively, a majority of all the votes cast being necessary to a choice.

G. L., ii, 1, 6.

105. Nominations are to be made at the meeting at which the election is held, and at the preceding meeting.

G. L., ii, 4.

107. Soliciting votes for office is forbidden.

G. L., ii, 4.

108. Vacancies are filled in the manner of the original election.

G. L., ii, 8.

109. No one, except a past chancellor or a past vice chancellor, is eligible to election as chancellor commander; and no one, except a past chancellor or a knight who has served one term as an officer, is eligible to election as vice chancellor. If all qualified decline to serve, any knight who has been a member of the lodge for twelve months may be elected.

G. L., ii, 3.

The phrase "all qualified," above, includes only those who are present and nominated.

MS. decision of G. C., June 27, 1885.

110. Duties of officers prescribed.

G. L., iii.

111. Every officer elect must pledge himself, in open lodge, before installation, to memorize his portion of the ritual within six weeks thereafter. If this pledge be not fulfilled, the lodge may, without notice, declare the office vacant, and immediately fill the vacancy by election.

G. L., ii, 9.

112. The preceding section does not apply to the first term of a new lodge.

G. L., ii, 9.

113. Lodges may require the keeper of records and seal to perform the duties of master of finance, he giving a separate bond for the proper discharge of the duties of each office.

Jour. 1884, p. 184.

114. The master at arms has charge of the paraphernalia, and is responsible for its safe keeping.

G. L., iii, 8.

Installation.

115. The installation of an officer elect into an office to which he was not eligible under the law is null and void; and the grand chancellor has power to so declare,

and to direct the immediate election of some one who is eligible.

Jour. 1883, pp. 68, 96-7.

116. No one shall be installed into office who is indebted to the lodge.

G. L., ii, 5.

117. When an officer elect refuses to serve, after due notice of his election, the lodge should immediately declare the office vacant, and proceed to fill it after the manner of the original election.

Jour. 1881, pp. 448, 483-4.

118. The absence, without explanation, on the night of installation, of a member who was present when elected to office, is, in legal contemplation, a refusal to serve. The office should at once be declared vacant and filled by election.

Jour. 1883, pp. 68, 92.

119. It is the imperative duty of the deputy grand chancellor to see that every officer of the lodge shall pledge himself, in open lodge, before he is installed, to memorize his portion of the ritual within six weeks thereafter.

Jour. 1885, pp. 245, 295.

120. The installation of officers must take place on the first meeting night of each term, if practicable.

G. L., ii, 5.

121. A deputy grand chancellor may grant a dispensation for a public installation of officers. A dispensation from the grand chancellor is not necessary.

Jour. 1883, pp. 69, 96-7.

122. The deputy grand chancellor must install, or cause to be installed, the officers of his lodge.

Con., vi, 12.

123. A deputy grand chancellor, unable to be present at the time of installation, may appoint another past chancellor to perform that duty.

Jour. 1880, pp. 418-19.

124. An officer can not be installed except by the grand chancellor, the deputy grand chancellor or some past chancellor appointed by either for the purpose.

Jour. 1881, pp. 448, 483-4.

125. Installation of subordinate lodge officers, by a past chancellor who has not been

6

specially appointed to perform that service, is illegal.

Jour. 1885, pp. 240, 295.

126. Installation by a past chancellor, at the request of the deputy grand chancellor, is valid.

Jour. 1885, pp. 240, 295.

Honors.

127. The incumbent of an office at the end of a term is entitled to its honors.

G. L., ii, 8.

128. An officer who has been illegally installed is not entitled to the honors of the office, although he may have served until the end of the term.

Jour. 1877, pp. 272, 275.

Sitting Past Chancellor.

129. The retiring chancellor conmander shall fill the office of sitting past chancellor.

G. L., ii, 1.

130. If the chancellor commander be re-elected, an existing past chancellor must be elected sitting past chancellor.

G. L., ii, 1.

131. A retiring chancellor commander,

whether he was previously a past chancellor or not, is always the sitting past chancellor. If he is reelected and consequently does not retire, a sitting past chancellor must be elected from the roster of past chancellors.

Jour. 1884, pp. 183, 191, 193.

132. A retiring chancellor commander may resign the office of sitting past chancellor and be elected to another office.

Jour. 1874, pp. 66, 91.

133. At the institution of a new lodge, the office of sitting past chancellor must be filled by election.

G. L., ii, 7.

134. The sitting past chancellor is an officer and, as such, liable to be fined for absence.

Jour. 1875, pp. 126, 154.

This ruling was sustained by the supreme lodge, on appeal. (See supreme lodge journal 1876, p. 1306.)

135. A sitting past chancellor is liable to the same penalties for neglect of official duties as are imposed on other officers. A by-law which provides that any officer who is absent for a certain length of time shall forfeit his office, applies to the sitting past chancellor.

Jour. 1885, pp. 240, 295.

Chancellor Commander.

136. The chancellor commander gives the casting vote on all questions, except elections and appeals.

G. L., iii, 2.

137. It requires a majority vote to reverse a decision of the chancellor commander.

Jour. 1876, pp. 203, 226.

138. When a chancellor commander is personally cognizant of a violation of the laws of the order, it is his duty to proceed as directed by art. viii of the general laws, without waiting to receive " notice in writing of such violation."

Jour. 1880, pp. 391, 425.

Committees.

139. A subordinate lodge relief committee must consist only of the chancellor commander and the vice chancellor.

Jour. 1884, pp. 145, 185-6.

140. A committee to audit the accounts of the financial officers must be appointed by the chancellor commander, at the last meeting of the term.

G. L., iii, 2.

141. A "relief board," composed of members of different lodges, is extra-constitutional, and not amenable to the laws of the order in the expenditure of money.

Jour. 1880, pp. 391, 425, 427.

Conduct of Business.

142. At every regular meeting of a subordinate lodge, the lodge must be called to order, the roll of officers must be called, and a record of the meeting must be kept, whether or not a quorum be present.

Jour. 1885, p. 303.

143. In the absence of the chancellor commander and the vice chancellor, the senior past chancellor shall preside. If none be present, a knight may be called to the chair.

G. L., i, 4.

144. The actual business of the lodge must be transacted in the knight's rank.*

G. L., i, 5.

---

*See, as pertinent to this subject, Sec. 234 of this digest.

145. Discussion of political or religious questions in subordinate lodges is positively prohibited.

G. L., x, 5.

146. Each subordinate lodge must furnish the grand keeper of records and seal with an impression of its seal, to be kept on file in his office.

Con., vi, 5; G. L., vi, 1.

147. Communications to the grand chancellor, unless coming officially from the lodge, should not bear the lodge seal.

Jour. 1881, pp. 447, 483-4.

148. Each lodge is required to keep on file, in its castle hall, a complete set of the journals of the grand lodge.

Jour. 1875, pp. 142, 151.

Lodge Finances.

149. A lodge has the right to assess its members for necessary lodge purposes.

Jour. 1879, pp. 370-1.

150. A lodge has the right to assess its members to raise funds to pay its per capita tax.

Jour. 1880, pp. 390, 425, 427.

151. The grand lodge discourages the use of subordinate lodge funds in payment of the expenses of celebrations, parades, picnics, balls, etc.

Jour. 1878, p. 315.

152. A lodge has the right to appropriate its funds in payment of the expenses of a banquet; but the better plan would be to defray the cost of such entertainment by private subscriptions.

Jour. 1880, pp. 392, 425, 427.

153. All orders on the master of exchequer must be signed by the chancellor commander and the keeper of records and seal.

G. L., iii, 2, 5.

154. In the event of the death of the master of exchequer, the accounts of the master of finance will be sufficient vouchers.

G. L., iii, 8.

Benefits.

155. Each lodge has the right to determine whether or not benefits shall be paid at stated periods during sickness; and, also, whether or not members entitled to benefits shall be required to make formal application therefor.

Jour. 1881, pp. 483, 489.

156. A lodge can afford to pay, as weekly benefits, one-half the amount charged as annual dues.*

Jour. 1881, pp. 485, 488.

Dispensations.

157. A deputy grand chancellor may grant dispensations—

(*a*) To propose, elect and initiate at the same session. Fee, $2.

(*b*) To propose, elect and confer two ranks at the same session. Fee, $3.

(*c*) To propose, elect and confer the three ranks at the same session. Fee, $5.

(*d*) To confer two ranks at the same session. Fee, $1.

(*e*) To confer the three ranks at the same session. Fee, $2.

(*f*) To confer the ranks on a person over fifty years of age. Fee, $2.

Con., xii, 13.

158. A deputy grand chancellor can grant a dispensation to ballot on an application

---

* On the subject of the general relation of dues to benefits, a very able report, presented at the session of 1881 (journal, p. 485), may be consulted with profit.

for reinstatement at the session at which it is presented. Fee, $2.

Jour. 1884, pp. 145, 185-6.

159. When a dispensation is necessary to render an applicant eligible to membership, it must be procured before the application is ballotted on. A lodge can not elect an ineligible applicant, and afterwards procure a dispensation to initiate.

Jour. 1880, pp. 391, 425.

160. Dispensations to confer more than one rank at the same session, etc ., are granted to the lodge, and not to the individuals for whose benefit they are asked.

Jour. 1880, p. 419.

161. A dispensation from the grand chancellor or deputy grand chancellor is necessary for a lodge to make a public display, except on a funeral occasion.

G. L., x, 8.

162. All dispensations expire with the term of the officer who granted them.

Jour. 1880, p. 420.

Secret Work.

163. The representative of each subordi-

7

nate lodge is authority on all questions concerning the secret work which arise in his lodge during his term.

G. L., iii, 10.

164. Lodges have the option of conferring the third rank in either of the two forms prescribed in the ritual.

Jour. 1885, pp. 241, 295.

Petitions.

165. Petitions for initiation must be presented to the lodge nearest the petitioner's residence, unless the applicant obtain the permission of such lodge to petition elsewhere. In cities in which there is more than one lodge, an applicant may make choice of lodges.

Con., viii, 2.

166. The keeper of records and seal must notify all other lodges in the same town of the election or rejection of candidates, and of the reception of petitions for membership.

G. L., iii, 5.

Rank Fees.

167. The fees for the ranks shall not be

less than five dollars each (except for charter members of a new lodge).

G. L., iv, 1.

168. Every application must be accompanied by the fee.

G. L., iv, 1.

169. No rank shall be conferred, under any circumstances, unless the fee has been paid.

G. L., iv, 10.

170. The provision of the general laws, that "every application must be accompanied by the initiation fee," is mandatory; and it would be improper to read an application to the lodge unless the fee accompanies it.

Jour. 1881, pp. 448, 483-4.

Ballot on Petitions.

171. All ballots for ranks must be taken in the knight's rank.

Jour. 1887, pp. 245, 272, 275.

172. It requires a unanimous vote to elect a petitioner for any rank or for membership by card.

G. L., iv, 3, 5.

173. If the ballot on a petition be unfavorable, it must be renewed at once, without regard to the number of black balls cast.

G. L., iv, 3.

174. A quorum being present, the fact that only six votes were cast, in ballotting on a petition, is no ground for reconsideration, unless the ballot is explained as having been made through mistake.*

Jour. 1881, pp. 447, 483-4.

By-laws.

175. By laws of subordinate lodges are not in force until approved by the grand lodge, or, during recess, by the grand chancellor and the grand keeper of records and seal. There are various exceptions to this rule.

Con., xix.

176. The action of a lodge, in the adoption of new by-laws, must be governed by the requirements of the by-laws then in force.

Jour. 1883, pp. 69, 96-7.

---

*Query: Can reconsideration of a ballot be had, under any circumstances whatever, without contravening the spirit of the constitution of the supreme lodge (art. viii, sec. 2, subsec. 10)?

Miscellaneous.

177. Subordinate lodge castle halls will be dedicated by the grand officers, at the expense of the lodge.

Con., xviii.

178. The consent of the grand lodge is necessary to change the name of a subordinate lodge.

Jour. 1881, pp. 449, 483-4.

179. A duplicate charter should contain the names of all the original charter members, except those whose names were ordered by the grand lodge to be stricken off.

Jour. 1881, pp. 447, 483-4.

180. Paraphernalia may be improvised or manufactured by a lodge for its own use. Supplies must be procured from the supreme or grand lodge.

Jour. 1883, pp. 67, 96-7.

New Lodges.

181. The grand chancellor may, during the recess of the grand lodge, grant dispensations for the organization of new lodges.

Con., vi, 3.

182. When a charter is granted to a lodge,

the dispensation under which it was instituted must be returned to the grand keeper of records and seal.

Jour. 1875, p. 177.

183. Requisites for the organization of a new lodge.

Con., xiv.

184. The withdrawal cards of all members of the order who sign the application for a dispensation for a new lodge must be sent with the application to the grand keeper of records and seal.

G. L., vi, 6.

185. The charter fee for a subordinate lodge is twenty-five dollars.

Con., xii.

186. The charter fee of twenty-five dollars for a new lodge is to cover the cost of the charter and all supplies furnished by the grand lodge, except rituals and jewels.

Jour. 1884, pp. 145, 185-6.

187. A "set of supplies" for a new lodge shall consist of five rituals, four installation books, twenty-five ode cards, three music books, one bound volume of the grand lodge journal, [two bound volumes of the supreme lodge journal,] one grand lodge digest, one supreme lodge digest, one set of official jewels, one hundred official receipts and fifty copies of the constitution and general laws.

Jour. 1880, pp. 409, 417, 419.
Jour. 1881, pp. 460, 478-9.

Since the last session of the supreme lodge (journal 1884, p. 2985), copies of the supreme lodge journal are not part of a set of supplies for a subordinate lodge.

Since the promulgation of the revised ritual, a "question book" is necessarily part of a set of supplies.

188. On the institution of a new lodge, twenty-five dollars shall be paid from the grand lodge treasury to the person through whose efforts the lodge was organized.

Jour. 1883, pp. 100-101.

Defunct Lodges.

189. A subordinate lodge may be deprived of its charter for various causes.

Con., x, 1, 3.

190. A subordinate lodge can not surrender its charter so long as there are seven members who wish to retain it.

Con., x, 2.

191. The grand keeper of records and seal shall take charge of the property of defunct lodges, and go in person to secure possession thereof, whenever necessary.

Jour. 1878, p. 311.

192. After the lapse of two years, a dissolved or suspended lodge forfeits all right and title to its name and number and to the funds and effects surrendered to the grand lodge.

Con., x, 5.
G. L., x, 9.

193. A hall belonging to a subordinate lodge would not become the property of the grand lodge in case of the surrender or forfeiture of its charter.

Jour. 1883, pp. 68, 96-7.

194. A lodge may refuse admission to a committee from a lodge which has been suspended, and afterwards reinstated, official notice of the reinstatement not having been received by the first lodge.

Jour. 1878, pp. 293, 310-11.

III.--THE INDIVIDUAL MEMBER,

Admission.

195. Persons over fifty years of age may be initiated by dispensation.

> Con., xiii.
> G. L., iv, 1.

196. Persons under twenty-one years of age can not be initiated.

> G. L., iv, 1.

197. Maimed persons may be initiated by dispensation.

> G. L., iv, 1.

Dispensations for this purpose can be granted only by the grand lodge or grand chancellor. (See supreme lodge digest, 189.)

198. A man deformed by nature is not "maimed" in the sense in which the term is used by our laws. The word indicates the loss or injury of "some member useful in fight or flight."

> Jour. 1881, pp. 447, 483-4.

199. A man unable to write his name can not be initiated.

> G. L., iv, 1.

200. A member has no right to ask another how he will vote on a petition.

Jour. 1880, pp. 428.

201. A member has the right to make remarks when a petition is about to be acted upon, but not after the first ballot has been taken.

Jour. 1880, p. 428.

202. A rejected candidate for the first rank may petition again at the expiration of six months. A rejected candidate for the second or the third rank may petition again at the expiration of one month.

G. L., iv, 3, 10.

203. A member's reason for voting to reject a candidate can not be enquired into.

Jour. 1881, pp. 447, 483-4.

204. A member who has cast a black ball can not withdraw it, and the applicant can not petition again until the legal limit of time shall have expired.

Jour. 1882, pp. 8, 30.

205. Every elected petitioner, who fails to present himself for initiation or admission within six stated meetings after notification of election, unless unavoidably prevented, shall forfeit his fee.

G. L., iv, 8.

206. If objections to a candidate for any rank are presented after his election, and the objections are sustained by a two-thirds vote, he shall be excluded and his fee returned. G. L., iv, 12.

207. An applicant over fifty years of age may be admitted by card, on payment of the fee fixed by the lodge for admission by card, without extra charge on account of his age.

Jour. 1874, p. 93.

208. A brother who desires to again become a member of a lodge from which he has withdrawn, can do so only in accordance with provisions of art. iv, sec. 5, of the general laws.

Jour. 1881, pp. 447, 483-4.

Pages and Esquires.

209. There is no prescribed time within which pages and esquires must apply for higher ranks. They forfeit no right by failing to do so.

Jour. 1885, pp. 241, 295.

S. A. P. W.

210. A member, to be entitled to the S. A. P. W., must be "clear of the books" up to the end of the preceding term, and under no charges.

Jour. 1874, pp. 88-9.

211. A "relief committee" has no right to demand the S. A. P. W. from a brother applying for aid.

Jour. 1879, pp. 327, 362.

Benefits.

212. To be entitled to benefits, a member must be entitled to the S. A. P. W.

G. L., v, 3.

213. A member who is not entitled to the S. A. P. W. is not entitled to benefits, although he may be less than one quarter in arrears for dues.

Jour. 1885, pp. 241, 295.

214. A member can not be debarred from sick benefits because he receives wages or salary during his sickness.

Jour. 1873, pp. 37, 39.

215. Holders of withdrawal cards are not entitled to benefits.

Jour. 1880, pp. 391, 425.

216. A member who withdraws by card does not thereby invalidate his right to benefits for sickness occurring before such withdrawal.

Jour. 1881, pp. 480-1.

217. A member can pay arrearages at any time, whether sick or well; and such payment places him "in good standing" and entitled to sick benefits from the date of payment.

Jour. 1884, pp. 145, 185-6.

218. A member can not be debarred from sick benefits, even if his sickness was caused by intemperance or immoral conduct, unless charges are preferred and proved.

Jour. 1884, pp. 145, 185-6.

219. Funeral benefits must be paid in full, and expenses incurred by the lodge in attending the funeral can not be deducted therefrom.

Jour. 1877, pp. 245, 272, 275.

Relief.

220. Cases of sickness or distress must be reported to the relief committee, without delay, by any member who hears of them.

G. L., x, 6.

221. Relief extended to the families of members is a matter of voluntary benevolence, and not the discharge of an obligation.

Jour. 1880, pp. 391, 425, 427.

Assessments.

222. Members of a lodge can not be exempted from the payment of funeral assessments levied by the lodge, on the ground that they are members of the endowment rank.

Jour. 1879, p. 355.

223. Charges should be preferred against members who refuse to pay assessments levied by the lodge.

Jour. 1880, pp. 390, 425, 427.

Fines.

224. A member can not be suspended for the non-payment of a fine.

Jour. 1881, pp. 448, 483-4.

The supreme lodge has since decided that lodges may provide for the suspension of members for the non-payment of fines legally imposed. (See supreme lodge journal 1884, p. 3063.)

225. A member who refuses to pay a fine

~legally imposed is liable to punishment for contempt.

Jour. 1881, pp. 481, 489.

Absentees.

226. A lodge has the right to fine or to prefer charges against a member who fails to attend a meeting to which he has been summoned.

Jour. 1885, pp. 241, 295.

227. It is not optional with a chancellor commander whether or not he will give a member permission to retire, and a member can not be required to give his reason for desiring to do so.

Jour. 1885, p. 303.

An appeal from this ruling to the supreme lodge has been taken.

Uniform.

228. A member has no right to wear any part of his Pythian uniform in a military company.

Jour. 1876, pp. 203, 226.

229. A Knight of Pythias must not lend any part of his uniform, or use it himself, for any other than a distinctively Pythian purpose.　Jour. 1879, pp. 328, 362.

Offences, Trials and Punishments.

230. Offences named, method of trial pre-scribed and punishments provided.

G. L., vii, 8.

231. A lodge has no power to fix any oth-er date than that prescribed by law for the trial of a member, until that date has ar-rived. If the accused or the lodge be not ready, another date may then be set—but not otherwise.

Jour. 1882, pp. 25, 31.

Appeals.

232. From the proceedings of a subordi-nate lodge any member has the right of appeal to the lodge.*

G. L., ix, 1, 2.

233. From all decisions of the presiding officer a member has the right of appeal to

---

* This is manifestly an error. The right of appeal from the proceedings of a subordinate lodge lies, of course, to the grand lodge. In the corresponding section of the original general laws (1872) the words "grand lodge" are used; and the substitution of "lodge" in the present code is doubtless due to an accidental omission by the printer of the first edition of the revision of 1875, which has been repeated in all subsequent editions.

the lodge. A majority may reverse his decision.

G. L., ix, 3.

234. Whenever a chancellor commander is violating the ritual, in any rank, a brother has the right to object, and, if it becomes necessary, appeal to the lodge, while in that rank.

Jour. 1883, pp. 105, 108.

This decision, on appeal to the supreme lodge, was reversed, that body holding that, "if a chancellor commander violated any of the provisions of the ritual, any brother would have the right to object; but the appeal from the decision of the chancellor commander could only be taken in the knight's rank." (Supreme lodge journal 1884, p. 3037.)

235. An appellant from the action of a subordinate lodge is liable for the cost of the transcript sent to the grand lodge.

Jour. 1874, pp. 66, 91.

Cards and Shields.

236. Subordinate lodges shall not charge less than one dollar for a withdrawal card.

G. L., vi, 8.

9

237. The fee for a duplicate withdrawal card, if the original has been lost, shall be fifty cents.

G. L., iv, 5.

238. A member can only withdraw from a lodge by withdrawal card.

Jour. 1876, p. 231.

Jour 1881, pp. 448, 483-4.

239. A withdrawal card must be granted, without vote, to an applicant therefor who is clear of the books, if no valid objection be made. If objection to granting the card be made, the member objecting must immediately state his reason; whereupon, the lodge shall decide by vote whether or not the card shall be granted.

Jour. 1876, pp. 203, 226.

240. The fee for a withdrawal card must accompany the application for the card.

Jour. 1881, pp. 448, 483-4.

241. A withdrawal card granted to a member not "clear of the books" is void.

Jour. 1880, pp. 390, 425.

242. The moment a withdrawal card is granted, it is constructively and *de jure* in possession of the applicant, and can be taken from him only in the manner prescribed by law. The mere clerical act of filling out and signing the card is not material.

Jour. 1880, pp. 390, 425.
Jour. 1881, p. 481.

243. If a withdrawal card is not deposited, it operates as a virtual severance of all connection with the order.

Jour. 1881, pp. 448, 483-4.

244. A withdrawal card can be used for transferring membership or severing connection with the order, only as prescribed by art. vi, sec. 3, of the general laws.

Jour. 1881, pp. 448, 483-4.

245. A brother to whom a withdrawal card has been granted, and the act of granting the card afterwards reconsidered, has no right to the S. A. P. W. The reconsideration was illegal, and he is not a member.

Jour. 1881, pp. 449, 483-4.

246. If a member who has applied for a withdrawal card withdraws his application before the card has actually been granted, his rights are not affected, and the card can not legally be issued. If it has been granted, and only awaits delivery, it is effective, and severs his membership.*

Jour. 1881, pp. 449, 483-4.

247. A lodge can not grant a withdrawal card to a member who has been suspended for non-payment of dues, without first re-instating him in accordance with law. Although he pay all dues and charges against him and apply for reinstatement, if he should be rejected on ballot, the lodge can not then lawfully grant him a card.

Jour. 1883, pp. 69, 96-7.

248. A member can not be required to pay dues beyond the time of making application for a withdrawal card.

Jour. 1885, p. 303.

249. Members of defunct lodges may obtain grand lodge cards, which can be used

---

* Query: When has a withdrawal card "actually been granted"? According to sec. 239, above, it must be granted "without vote"; and, according to sec. 242, "the moment it is granted," it is the property of the applicant, the mere act of delivery not being essential. Therefore, if the law has been complied with strictly, it would seem that there could be no opportunity, between the presentation of the application and the "actual granting" of the card, to withdraw the application.

as withdrawal cards in applying for membership in other lodges. Con., x, 6.

250. No travelling shield shall be used or recognized except that issued by the supreme lodge, and furnished by the grand lodge to the subordinate lodges for use by individual members. G. L., vi, 7.

251. Subordinate lodges shall not charge less than twenty-five cents for a travelling shield. G. L., vi, 8.

Suspension.

252. When a member is one year in arrears for dues, the master of finance must immediately notify the chancellor commander, who must, in open lodge, declare the delinquent suspended. Suspension for non-payment of dues is not operative unless the member in arrears has had notice, nor until the fact of suspension has been officially announced by the chancellor commander in open lodge.
G. L., v, 1; xii, 1.

253. A member can not be more than one year in arrears.
Jour. 1882, pp. 8, 30.

254. A member can not be suspended for

ninety-nine years, except for violation of the laws of the order and criminal violation of the laws of the land.

G. L., x, 2.

255. When a member has been suspended for ninety-nine years, the semi-annual returns must specify that the offender has been guilty of a violation of the criminal laws of the state as well as of the law of the order.

Jour. 1884, p. 191.

256. Any member who, when his lodge is suspended or dissolved, fails or refuses to deliver to the grand chancellor or his deputy any property or effects of said lodge in his custody, may be forever excluded from membership in the order.*

Con., x, 4.

Reinstatement.

257. Method of reinstatement prescribed.

G. L., xii, 2.

258. No member can be reinstated except by ballot.

Jour. 1881, pp. 447, 483-4.

---

* Art. x, sec. 3, of the general laws would seem to make the infliction of this penalty mandatory, so far as officers are involved.

259. A member suspended for non-payment of dues, applying for reinstatement, must pay one year's dues at the rate in force at the time of his suspension, notwithstanding the fact that a less rate is charged at the time of his application.

Jour. 1881, pp. 501-2.

260. A member to whom a withdrawal card has been granted but not delivered, and who, having been considered still a member of the lodge, has afterwards been suspended for non-payment of dues, can not be required, as a prerequisite to reinstatement, to pay the amount of dues charged against him. Granting the card severed his membership, and the subsequent suspension for non-payment of dues was illegal and void. (See sec. 242.)

Jour. 1882, pp. 8, 30.

261. An applicant for reinstatement, having been rejected, should have the amount paid by him at the time of application for reinstatement refunded.

Jour. 1884, pp. 145, 185-6.

262. A member suspended for non-payment of dues, and rejected on application for reinstatement, can apply again for reinstatement at any time thereafter.

Jour. 1884, pp. 145, 185-6.

263. When a lodge, by a two-thirds vote, after one week's notice, shall terminate the suspension of a member suspended for a definite time, he is thereby, without further action, restored to all his rights and privileges.

G. L., viii, 15, 16.

264. A member suspended for ninety-nine years can only be reinstated by vote of the grand lodge, on the unanimous recommendation of his lodge.*

G. L., x, 2.

265. A vote is required to reinstate a member at the expiration of his term of suspension.

Jour. 1876, p. 232.

This ruling was afterwards reversed by the grand lodge.   (Jour. 1884, pp. 152, 185-6.)

---

* This section seems to be inconsistent with the preceding, unless, indeed, the phrase "ninety-nine years" be understood to mean an *indefinite* length of time.

Alphabetical Index.

Section

ABSENTEES, GRAND LODGE—
When not entitled to per diem 46

ADMISSION—
Of persons over age 195, 207
Of minors 196
Of maimed persons 198
Of persons unable to write 199
After rejection 202
Time of application for 205
Objections to, effect of 206
By card 207, 208

ADVANCEMENT—
No limit as to time . . . . ▶ . 209

AGE—
Persons over fifty may be initiated 195
Persons under twenty-one not eligible 196

ALTERNATE REPRESENTATIVE—
Each lodge entitled to one 39
Time and manner of election 39
Must be a past chancellor 40

AMENDMENTS—
Of the constitution, how effected 63
Of the general laws, how effected 64

APPEAL—
Right of grand lodge to hear 5

10

APPEAL. (CONTINUED)— Section

Should be taken directly to grand lodge . . . 6

From decision of grand chancellor 50

From decision of deputy grand chancellor . . 84

From proceedings of subordinate lodge . . . 232

From decision of chancellor commander . . . 233

To be taken in third rank only 234

Cost to be paid by appellant 235

APPROPRIATIONS—

Vote required, in grand lodge 15

Vote required, in subordinate lodge 78, 79

ARREARAGES—

May be paid at any time 217

Maximum amount possible 233

ASSESSMENTS—

Lodge may make, for what purposes . . . 149, 150

No members exempt from payment 222

Method of enforcing payment 223

BALLOT ON PETITIONS—

Must be taken in third rank 171

Result must be unanimous 172

If unfavorable, must be renewed at once . . . 173

Defective 174

Questions concerning, improper 200, 203

Remarks before and after 201

BENEFITS—

Power of lodge as to payment 155

Relation of dues to 156

Title to, depends on S. A. P. W. 212, 213

Receipt of wages does not impair right to . . . 214

BENEFITS (CONTINUED)— Section
  Effect of withdrawal card on right to . . 215, 216
  Right to, how regained 217
  Immoral conduct forfeits, when 218
  Funeral, must be paid in full 219

BLACK BALL—
  One rejects 172
  Can not be withdrawn 204

BLANKS—
  Furnished to subordinate lodges 70

BOND—
  Of grand keeper of records and seal 34, 36
  Of grand master of exchequer 35, 36

BY-LAWS, SUBORDINATE LODGE—
  Must be approved before operative 175
  Method of adopting new 176

CERTIFICATE—
  Of past chancellor 3
  Of representative and alternate 39
  Of deputy grand chancellor 90

CHANCELLOR COMMANDER—
  Eligibility 109
  Gives casting vote, when 136
  Decision, how reversed 137
  Duty when law is violated 138
  Member of relief committee 139
  Must appoint auditing committee 140
  Must sign all orders 153
  Must give member permission to retire 227
  Reelected, becomes past chancellor, when . . 100

Section

CHANCELLOR COMMANDER, RETIRING—

Not eligible as representative 41
Becomes past chancellor, when 99
Not to be reported as past chancellor 101
Past chancellor elected in lieu of 102
Becomes sitting past chancellor 129, 131

CHARTER—

Can be granted only by grand lodge 4
Can be suspended only by grand lodge 4
Causes of forfeiture 75, 189
When it can not be surrendered 190
Names to appear on duplicate 179
Fee for 185, 186

COMMITTEES, GRAND LODGE—

List of 42
When appointed 43
On subordinate lodge by-laws 44

COMMITTEES, SUBORDINATE LODGE—

Relief, how composed 139
Auditing, how appointed 140

CONSTITUTION, GRAND LODGE—

How amended 63

DECISION—

Of grand chancellor 50
Of chancellor commander 233

DEDICATION—

Of castle halls 177

DEPUTY GRAND CHANCELLOR— · Section

One for each lodge 80
To be recommended by lodge 81
Grand chancellor may select 83
Grand chancellor may remove 80
Is authority on questions of law 84, 87, 88
May give official decisions, when 85
Decisions must be entered on records 86
Limit of judicial power 87
May hold office in subordinate lodge 89
Must file certificate of good standing 90
Must make official visits 91
Must forward returns promptly 92
Must make annual report 93, 94
May grant dispensations for what . . 121, 157, 158
Duties as to installation 122, 123, 124, 126

DISPENSATION—

Granted by grand chancellor 73, 197
Granted by deputy grand chancellor . 121, 157, 158
Must be procured before ballot 159
Granted to lodges only 160
Limit of existence 162
Necessary for public installation 121
Necessary for public display 161
For new lodge, how granted 181
For new lodge, when to be returned 182

DOCUMENTS, GRAND LODGE—

Requisites as to form, etc. 51

DUES, SUBORDINATE LODGE—

Relation of benefits to 156
Amount necessary for reinstatement 259

ELECTION—

Of grand officers 18, 19, 20, 21, 22, 23
Of representative and alternate 39
Of subordinate lodge officers 105

ELIGIBILITY—   Section
  Of grand officers 25
  Of representative and alternate 40, 41
  Of subordinate lodge officers 89, 109

ENTERTAINMENT OF GRAND LODGE—
  Recommendation concerning 11

ESQUIRE—
  Advancement optional 209

FINES—
  Penalties for non-payment 224, 225

FUNDS, SUBORDINATE LODGE—
  Should not be used for banquets, etc. . . 151, 152

GENERAL LAWS —
  How amended 64

GRAND CHANCELLOR—
  Appeal should not be taken to 6
  May consider appeal, when and how 7
  Invested with full power during recess 8
  May retain certain jewels 68
  May install subordinate lodge officers 124
  May grant dispensation for new lodge 181

GRAND KEEPER OF RECORDS AND SEAL—
  Amount of salary and bond 34
  Custodian of bond of retiring 36
  Annual report to be printed 38
  Duty as to defunct lodges 191

GRAND LODGE—
  (See " Lodge, Grand.")

GRAND LODGE CARD—
  May be used as withdrawal card 249

GRAND MASTER OF EXCHEQUER—
  Amount of bond 35
  Custodian of bond of retiring 36

HONORS OF OFFICE— Section
Who are entitled to 127
Illegal installation forfeits 128

HYPOTHETICAL QUESTIONS—
Not to be considered unless official 54

IMMORAL CONDUCT—
Only debars from benefits, when 218

INSTALLATION—
Of grand officers 24, 25, 26
Of subordinate lodge officers 120
Of ineligible officer, void 115
Of delinquent, forbidden 116
Effect of officer's absence from 118
Public, dispensation necessary for 121
Who may perform 122, 123, 124, 126
By unauthorized past chancellor, illegal . . .125
Illegal, forfeits honors 128

JEWELS, GRAND LODGE—
Not to be retained by grand officers 68

JOURNAL, GRAND LODGE—
Who are entitled to copies 69
Lodges must keep on file 148

KEEPER OF RECORDS AND SEAL—
May act as master of finance 113
Must sign all orders 153
Duty as to petitions 166

KNIGHT—
May preside, when 143

LODGE, DEFUNCT—
Disposition of property of 191
Limit of claim to property 192
Hall does not revert to grand lodge 193
Rights of members of 194
Members may obtain grand lodge cards . . .249

LODGE, GRAND— Section

Who are members of 1
Powers of 4, 5
Annual sessions of 9
Invitations to, how referred 10
Recommendation as to entertainment of . . . 11
Quorum 12
Voting in the 13, 14, 15, 17, 20, 21, 22, 23
Yeas and nays 16
Officers 18
Committees 42, 43, 44
Regalia to be worn in 47
Parliamentary guide of 48
Order of business 49
Questions of order in 50
Form of documents 51
Hypothetical questions 54
Dues from subordinates . . . . 55 to 62
Amendments of constitution 63
Exemplification of secret work 65
Seal, when not to be used 67
Jewels, restrictions as to use 68
Journal, how distributed 69

LODGE, NEW—

Dispensation for, how granted 181
Charter, how granted 4
Requisites for organizing 183
Cards of members to be deposited 184
Charter fee 184, 185
Set of supplies for 187
Compensation for organizing 188
Fees of charter members 167
When chartered, must return dispensation . . 182
Must elect sitting past chancellor 133
Officers exempt from pledge 112

LODGE, SUBORDINATE—

Composition of 72

LODGE, SUBORDINATE (Continued)— Section

Must meet weekly 73, 76
Special meetings 74
Penalty for failure to meet 75
Quorum 77
Vote necessary for appropriation 78, 79
Officers . . . . 105 to 114
Committees 139, 140
Essentials of every meeting 142
Presiding officer 143
Business transacted only in third rank . . 144, 234
Political and religious discussions forbidden . 145
Certain duties prescribed 146, 148
May assess its members 149, 150
Recommendations as to funds 151, 152
Power as to benefits 155
Relation of dues to benefits 156
Option as to third rank 164
Petition must be presented to nearest 165
When petitioner has choice of 165
By-laws 175, 176
Dedication of castle hall 177
Change of name 178
May make paraphernalia 180
Causes of forfeiture of charter 189
Charter can not be surrendered, when : . . . 190

MAIMED PERSON—
May be admitted by dispensation 197
Meaning of the term 198

MASTER AT ARMS—
Responsible for paraphernalia 114

MASTER OF EXCHEQUER—
Orders on, by whom signed 153
Vouchers in case of death of 154

MASTER OF FINANCE—
Keeper of records and seal may act as 113
Accounts are vouchers, when 154

11

MEMBER—   Section
  Charter, fee of 167
. Has a right to retire 227
  Restrictions as to uniform 228, 229
MILEAGE AND PER DIEM—
  Of grand officers and representatives 45
NAME OF LODGE—
  How changed 178
OBJECTIONS—
  To admission of candidate 206
OFFENCES—
  What are 230
OFFICERS, GRAND—
  Eligibility 25
  Election of 18, 19, 20, 21, 22, 23
  Penalty for soliciting votes for 27
  Installation of 24, 25, 26
  Duties of 28, 33
  Vacancies, how filled 29
  Rights of 30
  How removed from office 31
  May be suspended 31
  Can not officiate while on trial 32
  Entitled to mileage and per diem 45
OFFICERS, SUBORDINATE LODGE—
  Time and mode of election 105
  Nominations 106
  Vacancies, how filled 108
  Duties of 110
  Pledge required before installation . . . 111, 119
  Installation, when void 115
  Installation, when forbidden 116
  Effect of refusal to serve 117
  Effect of absence from installation. 118
  Time of installation 120
  May be publicly installed 121
  Who may install 122, 123, 124, 126

OFFICERS, SUBORDINATE (Continued)— Section
Who may not install 125
Title to honors 127, 128

ORDER OF BUSINESS—
In the grand lodge 49

ORDER, QUESTIONS OF—
Must be decided without debate 50

PAGE—
Advancement optional 209

PARAPHERNALIA—
Master at arms has charge of 114
May be made by lodge 180

PARLIAMENTARY LAW—
"Robert's Rules of Order" adopted 48

PAST CHANCELLOR—
Member of the grand lodge 1
Who may receive the rank 2
Requisites of admission to grand lodge 3
May vote in election of grand officers 20
Representative and alternate must be 40
Lodge entitled to one for each term 95
Can not be elected to fill vacancy 96
Three to be elected by new lodge 97, 98
When retiring chancellor commander becomes. 99
When reelected chancellor commander becomes.100
In lieu of retiring chancellor commander . . . 102
Emeritus, rights and privileges of 103
Emeritus, need not have received rank 104
Retiring chancellor commander not to be report-
ed as .101
May install officers, when 123, 124, 126
May not install officers, when 125

PAST GRAND CHANCELLOR—
Member of the grand lodge 1
May vote in the grand lodge 13

PENALTY—   Section

For failure to pay grand lodge dues 61, 62
For failure to hold lodge meetings 75
For soliciting votes in grand lodge 27
For non-payment of assessments 223
For non-payment of fines 224, 225
For failure to obey summon 226
For failure to surrender lodge property 256
For various offences 230

PER CAPITA TAX—

To be fixed at each session 55
What lodges are not liable for 56
What members new lodges are liable for . . . 57
Penalties for failure to pay 61, 62

PETITION—

Must be presented to nearest lodge 165
Option of applicant as to 165
Lodges in same town to be notified of 166
Must be accompanied by fee 168
Must not be read without fee 170
Questions as to vote on, improper 200, 203
Renewal of, after rejection 202, 204

POLITICAL DISCUSSION—
Positively prohibited 145

POSTPONEMENT, INDEFINITE—
Effect of, in grand lodge 52

PRESIDING OFFICER—
Majority may reverse decision 233

PUBLIC DISPLAY—
Dispensation necessary for 161

PUBLIC INSTALLATION—
Dispensation necessary for 121

QUORUM—

Of the grand lodge 12
Of a subordinate lodge 77

RANK— Section
Option as to third 164
Must not be conferred until paid for 169
Ballot on petition for 171, 172
RANK FEE—
Minimum 167
Must accompany petition 168, 170
No rank to be conferred without 169
RANK TAX—
To be fixed from time to time 58
Takes effect, when 59
Fifteen members of new lodge exempt 60
Penalties for failure to pay 61, 62
REFERENCE OF DOCUMENTS—
Not to be considered unanimous consent . . . 53
REGALIA—
To be worn by representatives 47
REINSTATEMENT—
Application may be balloted on at once . . . 158
Method of 257, 258, 263, 264, 265
Amount to accompany application 259
Of member erroneously suspended 260
Payment by rejected applicant to be refunded . 261
May be applied for at any time 262
REJECTION—
Renewal of petition, after 202, 204
Questions concerning, improper 203
RELIEF—
Duty of members concerning 220
Obligatory to members only 221
RELIEF BOARD—
For the grand jurisdiction 33
Of subordinate lodges, extra-constitutional . . 141
RELIEF COMMITTEE—
Composition of 139
Can not demand S. A. P. W 211
Sickness or distress to be reported to 220

RELIGIOUS DISCUSSION—   **Section**
Positively prohibited 145
REPORT—
Of supreme representatives . . . . ' . . . 37
Of grand chancellor 38
Of grand keeper of records and seal 38
Of deputy grand chancellor 93, 94
REPRESENTATIVES, GRAND—
Each lodge entitled to one 39
Time and manner of election 39
Must be a past chancellor 40
Retiring chancellor commander not eligible . . 41
Entitled to mileage and per diem 45
Regalia to be worn by 47
Is authority on secret work 163
REPRESENTATIVE, SUPREME—
Election of 18
Report to be printed 37
RETIRE—
Member has a right to 227
RETURNS, SEMI-ANNUAL—
Must be forwarded within thirty days 92
Concerning suspensions for cause 255
RITUAL—
Officers to memorize parts of 111, 119
Appeal from violation of 234
SALARY—
Of the grand keeper of records and seal . . . 34
SEAL, GRAND LODGE—
Not to be affixed to unofficial documents . . . 67
SEAL, SUBORDINATE LODGE—
Impression to be furnished the grand keeper of
   records and seal 146
Unofficial communications not to bear 147
SECRET WORK—
Exemplification in grand lodge 65
Representative is authority on 163

S. A. P. W.—   Section
   Lodge to be deprived of, when 62
   Deputy grand chancellor to receive, when . . 90
   Who are entitled to 210
   Benefits depend on title to 212, 213
   Relief committee can not demand 211

SESSIONS—
   Of the grand lodge 9
   Of subordinate lodges 73, 74, 75, 76

SITTING PAST CHANCELLOR—
   Office, how filled 129
   Elected, when 130, 131, 133
   May resign 132
   May be fined for absence 134
   Liable to same penalties as other officers . . . 135

SOLICITING VOTES—
   In the grand lodge 27
   In a subordinate lodge 107

SUMMON—
   Penalty for failure to obey 226

SUPPLIES—
   Prices of 71
   How procured 180
   To be furnished new lodges 186, 187

SUSPENSION—
   Lodges to be notified of 66
   For non-payment of dues 252
   For cause 254, 255, 256

THIRD RANK—
   Form of conferring, optional 164
   All ballots for ranks must be taken in 171

TRAVELLING SHIELD—
   Only official to be used 250
   Minimum price of 251

TRIAL—
   Form and method of 230
   Postponement of, how effected 231

UNANIMOUS CONSENT— Section

Not implied by reference without objection . . 53

UNANIMOUS VOTE—

Required to elect a petitioner 172

UNIFORM—

Must not be worn in military company 228

Must not be lent 229

VACANCIES—

In grand lodge offices 29

In subordinate lodge offices 108

VICE CHANCELLOR—

Eligibility 109

Shall preside, when 143

WAGES—

Receipt of, does not forfeit benefits 214

WITHDRAWAL CARD—

To be filed by charter applicant 184

Holder not entitled to benefits 215

Holder entitled to former benefits 216

Minimum price of 236

Price of duplicate 237

Is the only method of withdrawal 238

When and how obtained 239

Fee must accompany application for 240

Void if granted to delinquent 241

Delivery not essential 242, 260

Effect, if not deposited 243

Can only be used as prescribed by law 244

Granting can not be reconsidered 245

Effect of withdrawal of application 246

Can not be granted to suspended member . . . 247

Payment of dues to obtain 248

Use of grand lodge card in lieu of 249

WRITE, INABILITY TO—

Renders applicant ineligible 199

www.ingramcontent.com/pod-product-compliance
Lightning Source LLC
Chambersburg PA
CBHW020047030726
47499CB00007B/2617